THIS BOOK
BELONGS TO

___ ___ ___ ___ ___ ___ ___ ___ ___ ___ ___ ___

___ ___ ___ ___ ___ ___ ___ ___ ___ ___

Published by BBC Books,
an imprint of BBC Worldwide Publishing.
BBC Worldwide Ltd., Woodlands, 80 Wood Lane, London W12 0TT

First published 1955 by Sampson Lowe

This edition 1992
Reprinted 1994, 1995
© Darrell Waters Limited 1955 as to all text and illustrations

Enid Blyton's signature mark and the word 'NODDY'
are Registered Trade Marks of Darrell Waters Limited

ISBN 0 563 36819 5

Printed in Great Britain by BPC Paulton Books Limited.

YOU FUNNY LITTLE NODDY

BY Enid Blyton

CONTENTS

BBC BOOKS

"IT DOESN'T MATTER IF IT'S TOO BIG, IT WILL KEEP YOU
DRY," SAID BIG-EARS

6

1

IT'S RAINING

PITTER-PATTER, splish, splash, drip-drip-drip!
Pitter-patter, splish-splash . . .

Whatever was that noise? Noddy woke up with a jump. He sat up in bed, rubbing his eyes.

Pitter-patter, pitter-patter, drip-drip, splash, splish . . .

"Goodness—it's raining!" said little Noddy. "I quite thought I must have left my tap dripping." He jumped out of bed and ran to the window. He could hardly see out of it because of the raindrops running down the pane.

Noddy sang a little song:
"I really love a rainy day,
  With puddles in the street,
  And raindrops bumping on my nose,
  And splishy-splashy feet!
  I wish I were a little duck
  That didn't wear a mac,
  I'd like to feel the raindrops run
  All down my feathery back!
  I really love a—"

A loud knock came at the door and made
Noddy jump. "Milko!" said a voice, and the door
opened. There stood the milkman, dripping wet
from head to foot.
"I won't come in and
tap your head

8

to make it nod this morning," said the milkman. "I'm too wet. Noddy, hurry and dress yourself. It's so wet this morning that there will be lots of people who will want to hire your car!"

"Oooh, yes! I hadn't thought of that," said little Noddy. "Here I am still in my pyjamas. Do you like them, milkman?—They're new."

"Very nice," said the milkman, and off he went next door to Mrs Tubby Bear's house.

Noddy dressed himself in a hurry. "I shall make a lot of money today," he thought. "People don't like walking in the rain, especially those with tails, like Miss Fluffy Cat, or Mr Monkey. They get them so wet."

He cleaned his teeth and washed himself. Then he cleaned his teeth again.

"I forgot to clean you last night, teeth," he said.

9

"That's why I'm cleaning you twice this morning. Now, where's my hair-brush? Hair-brush, where are you? Oh yes, I remember, I put you inside my hat. Did you have a nice cosy night there? Now for my breakfast."

Noddy got out his little car after breakfast and had a good look at it. "You're dirty," he said. "Very dirty. The rain will wash you clean. Good gracious me, I shall get very wet today. I really ought to buy myself a mac."

He was just driving his little car out of the gate when somebody came down the road on a bicycle, ringing his bell loudly. Ting-a-ling-a-ling!

"Big-Ears! Have you come to see me?" called

Noddy, very pleased to see his friend. "I'm just going out to get some passengers in my car. I shall get a lot today because it's so rainy."

"Yes, I know. I've come to lend you my old mac," said Big-Ears, getting off his bicycle. "I've got a new one, and I thought of you out in the rain today, so I've come to lend you my old one."

"It will be much too big," said little Noddy. "Oh, Big-Ears, what a most bee-yoot-iful new mac you've got, with a belt, too! I'd like one like that."

"Well, you work hard today and you'll be able to buy one," said Big-Ears. "Get out of the car and put this old mac of mine on. Come along now, no fussing! It doesn't matter if it's too big, it will keep you dry."

Little Noddy had to do as he was told when Big-Ears spoke in such a firm voice, so he got out of his car and put on Big-Ears' old mac. It came right down to his feet! He does look rather

11

peculiar in the picture, doesn't he?

"Turn back the cuffs," said Big-Ears, "then you can drive all right. And don't look so cross. You should smile at me and say 'thank you', not frown like that."

"Thank you, Big-Ears," said Noddy. "But I don't really like your old mac. Everyone will laugh at me."

Big-Ears went off in a huff, looking enormous in his grand new mac. Noddy drove off to look for passengers. Parp-parp! Who would be the first?

2

A LITTLE ACCIDENT

"HEY!" called somebody, as Noddy drove round the corner. "Stop, Noddy! I want to hire your car to take me to the market."

It was Mr Wobbly-Man. Noddy got out to help him into the car, because Mr Wobbly-Man had no feet.

"It's no fun for me on a rainy day," said Mr Wobbly-Man. "I wobble into all the puddles and get all splashed and muddy. What's that peculiar thing you've got on, Noddy? Is it an old dressing-gown?"

"No. It's Big-Ears' mac," said Noddy. "I don't like it. The cuffs keep coming over my hands so that I can't steer properly. Ooooh—what a wobble the car gave then—I'll be on the pavement next time if I'm not careful!"

"How rainy it is," said the Wobbly-Man. "Noddy, that mac is so big that you could really let me share half of it. Stop and see if it will go round us both."

Noddy stopped and soon the old mac was round both him and the Wobbly-Man. "Ah—that's better," he said. "I'll pay you double-fare, Noddy. This is fine."

But it was very difficult to drive when somebody else was wearing the same mac, and suddenly Noddy's car swerved again—and knocked down a lamp-post.

"Oh dear—now we've *both* got to get out and put up that lamp-post again," said Noddy, "because we're wearing the same mac. Wait a minute—there's Sally Skittle. I'll ask her to put up the lamp-post for me."

He leaned out of his car. "Sally Skittle! Please could you stand up that lamp-post for me?"

Sally Skittle kindly stood it up—and, will you believe it, Noddy's car knocked it over again as soon as it started off! Bang! Down it went.

And then Mr Plod came up, frowning. "*I* saw you knock that lamp-post down as soon as kind Mrs Skittle stood it up, little Noddy. I shall charge you sixpence for making yourself a nuisance. Bring me the money tonight."

"I didn't mean to knock it down," said poor Noddy. "I didn't, I didn't, I didn't, I di . . ."

"I shall charge you a penny for each 'didn't' if you're not careful," said Mr Plod, crossly.

"Come on, little Noddy," said the Wobbly-Man. "It's no use arguing with Mr Plod. I want to get to the market."

They were soon at the market. Most of the stalls had umbrellas over them, very nice ones, striped and coloured. Noddy wished he had one for his car!

It was quite a difficult job to get Mr Wobbly-Man out of Big-Ears' mac. He paid Noddy double-fare, and wobbled away to do his shopping. Noddy pulled the big mac round him again. Oh dear, he felt quite lost in it.

A LITTLE ACCIDENT

Mrs Minnie Monkey hurried up to him. "Oh Noddy! Please will you drive me home. I'm getting my feet so wet!"

She got in and took hold of her tail so that it wouldn't hang from the car. "Do you mind if I put it on your knee, Noddy?" she said. "I've no room on mine because of my shopping basket."

She swung her tail up on his knee. Noddy didn't like it at all. He put it back beside Mrs Monkey. "It's a very wet tail," he said. "It's dripping through the opening of my mac and making my legs wet. Keep it on your side of the car, Mrs Minnie, please."

MRS MONKEY SWUNG HER TAIL UP ON NODDY'S KNEE

But in half a minute the tail was on his knees again, drip-dripping all over him. Noddy was cross. He took it in his left hand and stuffed it firmly into Mrs Monkey's shopping-basket. She whisked it out angrily.

"Don't do that! Wetting my cakes and my sugar! Let me put it into your mac pocket. It's big enough."

"No," said Noddy and pushed the wet tail away. "I tell you, I don't like your tail, Mrs Minnie."

The car wobbled when he took his hand from the wheel and crashed into a little red post-box standing at the side of the road. Over it went and began to roll away, all the letters spilling out of it.

"Look at that now!" said Noddy, crossly. "That was your fault, Mrs Minnie. Please get out and put the post-box up again and post the letters in it."

"Certainly not," said Mrs Monkey. "My goodness, it's rolling down the hill—look! You'd better catch it, Noddy!"

Well, Noddy had to get out of the car then, his big mac almost tripping him up. He ran after the red post-box that was now rolling quite fast down the hill. Everyone was jumping out of the way.

Bump! It knocked into someone and down he went. Oh goodness gracious, it was Mr Plod the policeman! There he was in the road, trying to push the red post-box off himself.

"Who did this?" he roared angrily. Little Martha Monkey pointed her finger at Noddy.

20

"*He* did! He rolled it all the way down the hill and knocked you over with it, Mr Plod! He did!"

"Ooooh, I didn't," said Noddy. "I didn't, I didn't, I di . . ."

"Oh—it's *you* again, is it?" said Mr Plod in such a stern voice that Noddy left the post-box where it was and scuttled back to his car in fright.

"You come back!" shouted Mr Plod. "I shall fine you one shilling for knocking me over with the post-box, and one shilling for emptying out the letters and—"

But Noddy didn't wait to hear any more. He drove off at top speed and never even noticed that he was sitting on Mrs Monkey's wet tail. She was very annoyed.

"Will you get off my tail, Noddy? Noddy. STOP! You're sitting on my TAIL!"

Noddy stopped when he was safely round a corner. He glared at poor Mrs Minnie Monkey. "I will NOT have that tail of yours in my car any more," he said. "Take it out of my car."

"Very well, I will," said Mrs Monkey, and got out with her shopping. "If my tail goes, I go too—and we shall *not* pay you a penny, Noddy. In fact I shall complain to Mr Plod."

"No. Don't do that!" called Noddy in alarm. But Mrs Monkey had gone off in a temper.

"Oh dear—this isn't my lucky day!" said little Noddy, and on he drove again.

3

EVERYTHING'S GOING WRONG

SOON Mrs Cat hailed him. "Noddy! Take me to the cake-shop. I've got to meet my sister there and I really can't walk all through these puddles."

Mrs Cat got into the car. She had an umbrella with her and held it over both of their heads.

"I don't think I want to go right to the cake-shop," said Noddy. "It's opposite the police-station and Mr Plod is very cross with me this morning."

"Don't be silly. You're a taxi-driver, aren't you?" said Mrs Cat. "Well, you have to go where your passengers tell you to go. Drive to the cake-shop."

Noddy drove off carefully. Mrs Cat saw someone she knew across the road and waved her umbrella at her friend.

"Don't do that," said Noddy. "Your umbrella nearly went into my eye. You can't wave umbrellas about in cars."

"Keep your eye out of the way then," said Mrs Cat. "Oh dear—it's raining harder than ever." She put the umbrella right in front of her face—and Noddy's too—to stop the rain from wetting her hat.

Noddy couldn't see at all, of course. He stopped the car at once and glared at Mrs Cat. "How can I see through an umbrella?" he said. "Take it away from my face."

"How fussy you are this morning, Noddy," said Mrs Cat, surprised. "Not a bit like yourself. If you feel like that I'll just put the umbrella down and get wet!"

Noddy drove on while Mrs Cat tried to put the umbrella down. Just as they came to the cake-shop the umbrella was caught by the wind and pulled out of Mrs Cat's hands—whoooosh!

Noddy was so surprised that he ran straight into a fruit-barrow just in front of him.

Crash! Bang!

24

NODDY WAS SO SURPRISED THAT HE RAN STRAIGHT INTO A
FRUIT-BARROW JUST IN FRONT OF HIM!

Over went the cart, and apples and oranges rolled about all over the place. "Oh!" squealed Mrs Cat, and "Hey!" shouted Mr Tom Teddy, whose barrow it was.

Noddy was just getting out of the car to help pick up the oranges and apples when he saw the door of the police-station opposite opening—and out came Mr Plod to see what the crash was.

Poor little Noddy! He got back into his car very quickly indeed. "I didn't, I didn't, I didn't MEAN to!" he shouted at Mr Plod.

26

EVERYTHING'S GOING WRONG

Oh dear—now Mrs Cat was telling Mr Plod how she had lost her umbrella, and Mr Tom Teddy was complaining bitterly.

Noddy began to sing very sadly indeed.

"What an unlucky day,
Everything's going wrong!
I think I will run away,
So, little car, hurry along!
Nobody likes me at all,
Everyone's cross as can be,
I feel very little and small,
I really am sorry for Me,
I—really—am—sorry—for—ME!"

4

THE PUDDLY STREET

NODDY soon found himself in a very puddly road indeed. "I'll cheer us up, little car," he said. "We'll drive into all the Very Biggest Puddles, and make Great Big Splashes."

So he and the car had a wonderful time in that puddly road. "Here's a fine big puddle!" said little Noddy, driving straight at it. "Whoooosh! In we go!"

My goodness me—what a splash they made!

"That was like a fountain," said Noddy, feeling much better. "Here's another big puddle, car—in we go!"

And in they went at top speed. Splash!

"That puddle was almost like a little pond," said Noddy. "Could you do a *bigger* splash still, do you think? Perhaps you could if you did a little *jump*, car!"

28

The car was enjoying itself as much as Noddy was. It ran at the next puddle at top speed and gave a jump in the air. WHOOOOOSH! Down it went into the muddy puddle—and there it stayed! It was stuck. It couldn't get out.

And then came the sound of angry voices from two people on the nearby pavement. Noddy turned and saw Mr and Mrs Jumbo, covered with mud and water.

"Look what you've made your car do to us!" cried Mr Jumbo, shaking himself so that drops of water flew everywhere. "We were just walking along quietly, trying not to get into any puddles—when along you come with your car, and splash, you jump into the very biggest puddle, and here we are, covered with mud from head to foot."

"I'm sorry, I'm sorry, I'm sorry," said little Noddy, trying to make his car get out of the puddle. "I didn't mean to, I didn't, I didn't, I didn't, I—"

And of course, just at that very moment, who should come walking round the corner but Mr Plod! Noddy gave a yell, leapt out of his car and ran away.

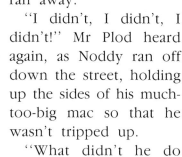

"I didn't, I didn't, I didn't!" Mr Plod heard again, as Noddy ran off down the street, holding up the sides of his much-too-big mac so that he wasn't tripped up.

"What didn't he do this time, Mr Jumbo?" asked Mr Plod. "Really, what is happening to little Noddy today? I'm always coming across him doing something naughty."

"Just look at us—wet from head to foot," said Mrs Jumbo. "I've got on my new hat too. That little Noddy wants a good telling-off, Mr Plod. That's what he wants."

Mr Plod took out his notebook and wrote in

"WHAT DIDN'T HE DO THIS TIME, MR JUMBO?" ASKED
MR PLOD

it in his best handwriting: "One good telling-off for Noddy."

"Right," he said. "I'll remember that. Now I'll get his car and take it to the police-station—and there it can stay till Noddy comes back again to fetch it. I'll be waiting for him."

But the little car didn't want to go with Mr Plod. It hooted loudly and suddenly shot forwards out of the mud. "Parp-parp!"
Where was it going to?

It was going to find Big-Ears to tell him to go and look for little Noddy. Noddy had run away! Where, oh where was little Noddy?

WHERE ARE YOU GOING
LITTLE NODDY?

NODDY ran round the street corner at top speed. He was too sad even to sing his Unlucky Song.

"Big-Ears went off in a huff this morning and he doesn't love me any more. I've knocked down a lamp-post. Mrs Minnie Monkey doesn't like me at all. I've knocked down a red post-box—and the post-box knocked down Mr Plod. Now what went wrong next?"

He ran on and on. "Oh yes, I remember. Mrs Cat lost her umbrella and I knocked Mr Tom Teddy's barrow over and *he's* cross with me too. Then I splashed Mr and Mrs Jumbo and they don't like me either. And Mr Plod is SIMPLY FURIOUS and will lock me up in prison. And I haven't even got my car."

Noddy began to cry. He looked up at the cloudy sky. "I'm raining too," he said. "I'm raining fast. My tears would make a very big puddle if I stood still, but I daren't in case Mr Plod catches me."

Noddy nodded his head sadly—but the bell at the top of his hat didn't ring—it didn't give even the tiniest jingle. Noddy took off his hat in alarm and looked at his little bell.

"Why don't you ring? Oh—you're dripping wet. You've lost your nice little jingle-jingle. You'll get rusty, little bell. I'll put you into the pocket of Big-Ears' mac and keep you dry."

34

So he pushed his blue hat into his pocket and went on his way again. He looked really very peculiar, with Big-Ears' mac down to his heels, and the cuffs hiding his little wooden hands. Noddy turned up the big collar.

"I don't like the rain trickling down my neck," he said. "I washed my neck well last night. Raindrops—you don't need to do it all over again!"

The funny little figure went on and on all alone, down this road and that. Pad—pad—pad. Where are you going, little Noddy? Where are you going?

35

6

EVERYONE IS WORRIED

Noddy's little car drove itself to Big-Ears' toadstool house and stood outside, hooting loudly. "Parp-parp."

Big-Ears was baking cakes. He shut the oven door and ran into the garden. "Noddy, is it you?"

But it wasn't Noddy. Only the car stood there giving tiny little hoots as if it wanted to say something important and couldn't.

"Take me to Noddy," said Big-Ears, jumping into the car and taking hold of the steering wheel. But the car stayed still. It didn't know where Noddy was. "Well, take me to Noddy's house then," said Big-Ears, impatiently, and at once the car started off and didn't stop till it came to Noddy's dear little House-for-One.

But nobody was there. Mrs Tubby Bear looked over the wall. "Are you looking for Noddy?" she said. "I'm afraid he has run away. I met Mr and Mrs Jumbo out this afternoon and they told me a lot of things about him."

"What did they tell you?" asked Big-Ears, looking very worried.

"Well, he wasn't very well-behaved today," said Mrs Tubby Bear. "He knocked down a lamp-post and he knocked over a red post-box, and he upset Mr Tom Teddy's barrow—and then he drove his car through a lot of big puddles and splashed Mr and Mrs Jumbo from head to foot."

"Good gracious me!" said Big-Ears, most surprised. "Whatever can have come over him? Do you suppose it was all his fault? He doesn't *usually* go about knocking so many things over."

"I think it must have been something to do with the rain," said Mrs Tubby. "And, of course, as Mr Plod was after him, as cross as could be, he got frightened."

"I'll stay in his house tonight and hope he comes back," said Big-Ears. "He's naughty sometimes, but he's very, very good at heart, Mrs Tubby."

"Oh, I know that," said Mrs Tubby. "We can't do without our dear little Noddy. I'm sure he didn't *mean* to do all those naughty things."

Well, Big-Ears stayed in Noddy's little house

all night long, but Noddy didn't come back. Big-Ears was so very worried. In the morning he went round to Mr Plod and told him that Noddy had disappeared.

38

BIG-EARS STAYED IN NODDY'S LITTLE HOUSE ALL NIGHT
LONG, BUT NODDY DIDN'T COME BACK

39

Then Mr Plod was worried. "Oh dear—I hope I didn't frighten him *too* much," he said. "He *was* tiresome yesterday, but I've found out since that Mrs Monkey was tiresome too, about her wet tail—and Mrs Cat was quite a nuisance with her umbrella in his car. I expect they upset little Noddy and made him drive into things."

"What are we to do?" asked Big-Ears. "We really must get him back. I shall miss him dreadfully. Toyland won't be the same without him."

"Well, there are only four roads he could have taken out of this town," said Mr Plod. "I will put out notices offering a reward to anyone who can say which one Noddy took. Someone will be sure to have noticed him."

So Mr Plod put out notices everywhere. They all said the same thing.

EVERYONE IS WORRIED

> LOST. LITTLE NODDY
> DRESSED IN BLUE HAT WITH BELL, RED
> SHIRT, BLUE SHORTS AND RED SHOES
> WITH BLUE LACES. YELLOW SCARF. A
> REWARD WILL BE GIVEN FOR ANY NEWS.

But, will you believe it, nobody came with any news at all. Big-Ears looked gloomier than ever, and everyone in Toy Town was worried as could be.

"We've driven him away because we were unkind to him," said Mrs Monkey, wiping her eyes.

"I didn't mean to be cross with him," said Mrs Cat, sniffing.

"Nor did we," said Mr and Mrs Jumbo. "Oh dear—we really DO miss little Noddy. Why don't we hear any news of him? Surely plenty of people must have seen him as he ran away?"

41

7

CLOCKWORK CAR TOWN

WELL, of course, plenty of people *had* seen him—but they didn't come and say so because they hadn't known it was Noddy that they met. Big-Ears and Mr Plod had forgotten that Noddy was wearing Big-Ears' old mac, and that his ordinary clothes couldn't be seen!

"We only met a funny little old man in a coat down to his ankles and his bare head buried deep in a turned-up coat-collar," said everyone. "We didn't see little Noddy in his blue, jingly hat and brightly-coloured clothes."

What was Noddy doing? Well, you'll never guess! He had gone on and on walking all through the night—and when day came he found himself in Clockwork Car Town.

CLOCKWORK CAR TOWN

Noddy was most surprised to see so many cars whizzing by him. One stopped near him and the driver called to him.

"Hey, little fellow! Wind up my car for me, will you? The clockwork has run down."

Noddy went up eagerly and turned the key until he could turn it no more. The driver liked the look of this little fellow in his blue hat and bright clothes, and gave him sixpence.

"Thank you!" said Noddy. He picked up Big-Ears' old mac from the ground where he had put it for the moment, and went on his way.

Noddy thought the little clockwork cars were lovely, but he did miss his own car. "Mine's better than these—it doesn't have to be wound up," thought Noddy. "Ah—here's another one run down. Sir, shall I wind up your car?"

"Thanks," said the man. "I'm going to the Great Car Race this afternoon. Are you going to watch it?"

"I don't know anything about it," said Noddy. "But I'd love to go."

"Meet me there, then," said the driver. "I am going in for the race—that is, if I don't feel too nervous! Aren't *you* going in for it?"

"No," said Noddy. "I'd love to, but I haven't got my car with me. I'll meet you there, sir."

"SIR, SHALL I WIND UP YOUR CAR?"

45

Well, Noddy wound up a lot more cars and earned quite a bit of money. Then he went to see the Great Car Race, and met the driver he had seen that morning.

Oh dear—he was shaking all over! "I'm all nervous again," he said to Noddy. "I shall never be able to hold the wheel. Will you drive my car in the race for me? I'll share half the prize money with you if you win."

"Ooooh—can I *really* go in for the race?" said Noddy, in delight. "In this lovely little car of yours? Right—I'll wind it up very, very carefully. I'm used to driving my own car—you just watch us go, sir!"

8

THE GREAT CAR RACE

ALL kinds of little clockwork cars began to line up for the race. Noddy's hat jingled loudly, he was so excited, and his head nodded up and down madly. "I do so wish Big-Ears could see me now!" he thought.

Bang! That was the starting signal. Off went the cars at top speed. R-r-r-r-r-r! R-r-r-r-r-r!

Noddy was fourth—then he crept up to third place—then to second! Now he was side by side with a fine big clockwork car driven by a sailor doll. How all the watching toys shouted in

47

excitement as the cars raced round and round the great ring.

"Faster, faster!" yelled everyone. "This is the last time round!"

Noddy yelled too, and his bell jingled loudly.

"Quick, little car, quick!" he cried. Hurrah! The car shot ahead and came in first, its clockwork *just* running down as it went past the winning post!

What excitement there was! Everyone crowded round little Noddy and clapped him on the back till he almost choked. "Who are you? What's your name?" they cried.

The owner of the car that Noddy had driven came striding up. He gave Noddy an enormous hug.

"You did it! You made my little car win the race! Well done, well done! Here's half

48

the prize money for you!'' And he poured so much money on to Noddy's lap that he could hardly believe his eyes!

"Oh no!" said Noddy. "Not all this!"

"Yes! I promised you half, you wonderful little fellow!" said the owner and patted Noddy and then patted the little car on its bonnet, too. "My word—I didn't know that my car could go so fast!"

Noddy was very pleased and very excited. He put the money into his pockets and how he clinked and jingled when he walked off! "I'll buy a present for Big-Ears," he thought. "I'll go back home now, because I've got enough money to pay Mrs Cat for her lost umbrella, and to get a present for Mrs Monkey because she was so upset about her tail."

He went on, jingling his money. "And I'll pay Mr Plod a lot because I knocked over a lamp-post and a post-box, and I'll pay Mr Tom Teddy for upsetting his cart. Oh yes—and I'll pay Mr and Mrs Jumbo for splashing their lovely clothes!"

After he had bought three big ice-creams for

himself, he set off back to Toy Town again. It would have taken him a long time, but a little wooden engine came trundling down the road and gave him a lift.

"You needn't drive me," said the engine. "I like going by myself. You can sit just behind my funnel if you like."

So Noddy sat behind the funnel and held on to it. The road was bumpy and Noddy jolted up and down, but he didn't mind. He was going home!

SO NODDY SAT BEHIND THE FUNNEL AND HELD ON TO IT

"I hope everyone will forgive me for being so naughty," he thought. "But I really didn't mean to be, I didn't, I didn't, I didn't."

He thought he would go and call at Mr Plod's first and pay him quite a lot of money. Then perhaps he wouldn't be cross with him any more. So he slipped off the little wooden engine just outside the police-station.

"Goodbye and thank you," he said. He put Big-Ears' old mac over his arm and walked over to the police-station. His bell jingled loudly as he knocked at the door. Blam, blam, blam—jingle, jingle, jingle!

9

HOW WONDERFUL!

NOW inside the police-station there were quite a lot of people, because everyone was feeling very, very worried about little Noddy running away. There was Mr Plod, of course, and Big-Ears and the Tubby Bears and Mr and Mrs Jumbo and Mrs Minnie Monkey and Mrs Cat, the Wobbly-Man, Mr Tom Teddy and quite a few others.

"We *must* find our little Noddy!" said Mrs Tubby. "I do miss him so!"

"I'll buy him a nice new mac," said Mr Jumbo. "Then he won't have to wear that enormous old one of yours, Big-Ears."

"And I'll buy him an umbrella—a big one that he can fix over his car when it rains," said the Wobbly-Man.

"I'll give him some of my oranges and apples," said Mr Tom Teddy. "But WHERE is he?"

There came a sudden knock at the door. Blam, blam, blam! And then another sound—a sound everyone knew and loved. Jingle, jingle, jingle!

"It's Noddy!" cried Big-Ears. "COME IN!"

The door opened and Noddy peeped in, scared to see so many people there. Oh dear—Mrs Cat, Mrs Monkey, the Jumbos, Mr Tom Teddy—they had all been so cross with him!

He stood there, his little wooden head nodding in excitement.

"I'm sorry, I'm sorry, I'm sorry!" he said, his voice squeaking in fright. "Don't be cross with me. Don't put me in prison, Mr Plod. Look, I've got enough money to pay you all for the naughty things I did!"

He put his hands into his pockets and pulled them out full of money. "I'll buy you a lovely present, Big-Ears," he said, "and for you, Mrs Cat, I'll buy—"

But he didn't say another word because Big-Ears had leapt up and run to him. He put his arms round little Noddy and hugged him like a bear.

"Little Noddy! Where have you been? We've worried such a lot about you!"

"We *are* so glad to see you," said Mrs Cat. "Welcome back!" said the Jumbos, and everybody said something nice and crowded round little Noddy to pat him on the back and hug him. Mr Plod came up too, smiling all over his red face.

Noddy ran to hide in a corner when he saw Mr Plod coming up. "Save me, Big-Ears!" he said. "Don't let him put me in prison!"

"I only want to hug you, you silly tiresome little rascal of a Noddy," said Mr Plod. "Now— where have you been?"

He gave Noddy a big hug.

HOW WONDERFUL!

"Dear me—isn't anybody cross with me any more?" said Noddy, in amazement. "Oh, I *am* glad. Well—I went to Clockwork Car Town and I drove in the big race there—and I won it! That's how I got all this money for you!"

"Good gracious! How *wonderful!*" cried everyone, and all at once Noddy was quite a hero. He beamed all over his little wooden face.

"We must tell EVERYONE this!" said Big-Ears in delight. "We always *knew* you were a good driver, Noddy, but we didn't know you could win races. Let's shout out the news in the market-place, and get everyone to cheer you!"

LITTLE NODDY IS HELD HIGH UP ON BIG-EARS' STURDY
SHOULDERS

HOW WONDERFUL!

So there they go, and little Noddy is being held high up on Big-Ears' sturdy shoulders. "Here comes Noddy, winner of the Great Car Race in Clockwork Car Town!" trumpeted Mr Jumbo, and everyone came running up to hear. "Here's our Noddy back again, covered with Glory!"

And now, who is this coming up too? "Parp-parp! PARP-PARP-PARP!" It is Noddy's little car.

"What, Noddy is back again? Noddy has driven *somebody else's* car? No, no, that won't do. He must drive his *own* car! Parp-parp-parp!" And as soon as Noddy saw his own little car, he leapt from Big-Ears' shoulders and jumped into the driving seat. Off he went, hooting loudly, and jingle-jingle went his bell.

What a lovely home-coming! Noddy isn't sad any more. He has plenty of money to spend on his friends, everybody loves him again and he's a real hero!

Mind that lamp-post, Noddy—be CAREFUL! Good gracious me, you made it wobble!

Oh what excitement!
What a grand day!
Noddy is home again,
Hip-hip-hooray!
There he goes driving
In his little car.
Home is our Noddy,
How happy we are!

THE NODDY LIBRARY